ACADEMY

SURFACE TO AIR

TOM PALMER

With illustrations by
David Shephard

First published in 2015 in Great Britain by
Barrington Stoke Ltd
18 Walker Street, Edinburgh, EH3 7LP

www.barringtonstoke.co.uk

Text © 2015 Tom Palmer
Illustrations © 2015 David Shephard

A CIP catalogue record for this book is available
from the British Library upon request

ISBN: 978-1-78112-398-0

Printed in China by Leo

To Lucas Craxford

ONE

Rory stared in horror from the back seat as the bus he was travelling in veered the wrong way round a roundabout. He closed his eyes, held onto the seat in front of him and waited for the collision.

A few seconds later, Rory opened his eyes again. Everything was fine. He was an idiot. And he knew it. He was just going to have to accept the fact that he was in France and French people drive on the wrong side of the road.

It wasn't the only new thing to get used to. The billboard ads flashing past were for products Rory couldn't place. And the music on the bus radio was all stuff he'd never heard before.

At home, when Rory and his mum had looked at the town of Toulon on a map, they'd seen that it was by the sea on the south coast of France. So Rory had expected it to be a place of beaches and palm trees. He had not expected warehouses and dual carriageways, traffic jams and beeping horns. Rory couldn't even tell his mum about it. She was thousands of miles away, working for the RAF in the Central Asian Republic. Or somewhere.

To clear his mind of his troubles, Rory scanned the horizon for rugby posts. If he saw rugby posts, he'd be able to imagine kicking the ball over them. And that would help him relax.

Rory's two best friends from school – Owen and Woody – were on the back seat next to him. The three of them were travelling with the rest of the school rugby team to take part in a tournament. Their school – Borderlands –

was representing the UK against a team from France, a team from Russia and a team from Italy. They were competing to be European Schools Rugby Champions.

When the bus came off the dual carriageway, Rory looked down at his map. They were heading into the centre of town now. Rory knew that he would get to see rugby posts very soon if they carried on this route, because the bus would head straight past the famous Stade Félix Mayol. It was one of the greatest rugby stadiums in Europe.

"Damn it," Rory heard the boy on the seat in front of him say. That was Jesse. Scrum half, star player, and Captain of Borderlands rugby team.

"What's up?" another voice asked. That was David, Jesse's friend.

"We're heading right, up into town," Jesse said. "If we'd gone left here we'd have seen the

harbour. My mum should be here by now. She
sailed out of Plymouth ten days ago."

"On your yacht?" David asked.

"Yeah," Jesse said. "The new one. The
Elite."

Rory looked back at his map and traced
the route of the bus with his finger as a way
to block out Jesse's voice. Jesse bothered
Rory. The idea that his family owned a yacht
bothered him too.

When Rory looked back up, he saw it across
a tangle of roads. The mighty Stade Félix
Mayol. Its stands towered over the road. There
was an arch at the corner of the stadium, with
the words –

VILLE DE TOULON – STADE MAYOL

On the other side of the arch, there was
a hint of green and two sets of posts. Rory
yearned to take a ball and start kicking there

4

and then. He half stood up to get a better view.
Then he saw Owen smiling at him – his friend
knew what he was thinking.

"Do you think they'd let me?" Rory asked.

"I doubt it," Owen said.

"Let him what?" Woody asked.

"Kick," Owen said. "On the pitch."

But Rory wasn't listening to his two friends.
He had his eyes closed now. In his mind he was
in the stadium and on the pitch. He let the ball
fall from his hands, kicked to send a drop goal
between those tall white posts.

TWO

Ten of the boys were watching a big TV screen in one of the hotel's meeting rooms when Rory, Owen and Woody joined them. The screen was filled with images of huge planes being loaded with brown boxes and bags of rice, followed by pictures of the same planes taking off down the runway at the RAF base back in England. A commentary in French ran in the background.

Most of the boys were familiar with these scenes. Borderlands was a boarding school and many of its pupils had parents in the RAF. That's why Rory's parents were away. His mum was an engineer who fixed damaged planes and helicopters. His dad supplied ammunition and spare parts to the army.

The boys watched the TV in silence. Most of them didn't understand the French news reader's commentary, but they were glued to the screen anyway. Rory could see that some of the adults were watching it in a worried sort of way too. He spotted David's mum, who had come to help with physio if any of the boys got injured. She was a sports doctor of some sort. David's sister, Taylor, was there as well, and they were both frowning at the screen. But they had every reason to look unhappy – it was only a few weeks since David's dad had been killed when an RAF plane went down over the Central Asian Republic.

"I'm not following this at all. It's too fast. What are they saying?" Rory heard Woody ask Owen.

"The war in the Central Asian Republic is now almost three months old ..." Owen translated from the French. "The British air force is lifting aid into the capital ... the rebels have the capital under siege ... The airlift is the only source of food for the 500,000 civilians trapped there ..."

Rory listened hard to every word to see if the news affected his parents.

"Hang on ..." Owen went on. "Many of the RAF planes have come under ... under fire." He began to look panicked. "The rebels are using ... I think they're saying 'surface-to-air missiles' ... Spaznyit ... something's being supplied by Russia ... the rockets, I think ... the British Prime Minister is in discussions with Russia to bring an urgent stop to this trade ..."

Woody looked at Rory. "I don't believe it," he said. "Do you mean that Russian arms dealers are supplying weapons to the rebels? What the ...?"

The room had filled up – all 20 players were now there to witness Woody's anger. Most of them were nodding in agreement. They all knew that Woody's dad was a Tornado pilot and

that he had good reason to fear surface-to-air missiles.

Then Mr Johnson came in – the head rugby coach and former Premiership second row was a big man. The boys fell silent as he walked up to the TV. He was joined by his assistant, Mr Searle.

"Please turn this off, boys," Mr Johnson said.

Three boys competed to grab the TV remote.

"Thank you," Mr Johnson said. "Right. We've got training in the morning. But I want to go through a few things. Some house rules. OK?"

When Mr Johnson's team talk had finished and everyone else headed to their rooms, Rory hung back and made for the stairway at the end of the corridor. He had something else to do before he went to bed. As he opened the door, a light flicked on. He walked down to the bottom floor, stretching his thighs and calves as he went. At the bottom, he turned round, checked his watch, took a deep breath, then ran hard up the stairs.

He checked his watch again as soon as he reached the sixth and top floor.

42 seconds.

Then, after a break, he went again.

39 seconds.

Better. But he would beat that by the end of the tournament. He'd get it down to 35. Maybe even 30. That was Rory's challenge to himself.

THREE

The next morning, after breakfast, Rory
followed the rest of the Borderlands squad
across the hotel lobby and onto a minibus.
They were going to the Toulon training ground
to prepare for the tournament.

As Rory stood outside in the rising heat, he
noticed that the air seemed to smell different
here. He could hear French voices coming
from an open window. Further up the road a
man was hosing the street. Rory watched the
rivulets of water snake towards the minibus.

Rory was struck by a clear memory of his
dad blasting the moss on the garden path at
the house on the airbase where they used to
live. He wondered where his parents were. He

hated the fact that he didn't know. He liked to look at the map in his diary and put his finger on where they were.

"Come on, boy," Mr Searle called. "On the bus."

The Toulon training ground was amazing. Superb. Nothing out of place.

After a good 15 minutes of warm-up, the Borderlands players ran in attacking formations, two groups of five going at each other. Then the backs were ready for a break. Mr Johnson asked Owen to hand out bottles of water to the others. The backs settled down to watch the forwards practising lineouts. The heat of the sun felt good.

"You're playing well," Rory said to Woody.

"I'm working on it," Woody replied.

Rory smiled. Just a few weeks had passed since Woody had arrived at Borderlands, saying he was into football and nothing else. He was so against the idea of playing rugby that he'd run away from the school on his first night there.

Rory saw Mr Johnson looking over at them and he grabbed his chance.

"Is it OK if I go and get some kicking done, sir?"

Mr Johnson smiled. "Yes, Rory. I'd expect nothing else."

Rory jumped to his feet and walked past the forwards to the posts. He bent to collect a ball from the pitch.

"Six from six," he said to himself, then felt for the notebook and pencil in his pocket. He'd record his success – or failure – there, like he always did. He'd also draw the path each kick followed. Then he would be able to look at his notes later and work out exactly where he could improve.

Rory set the rugby ball on the cone, put his right foot just under it, then stared at it.

As he stared he could hear two of his team-mates talking.

"Did you hear the Russian boys in the hotel reception?" one asked.

It was Jesse. No question.

"No," the other boy said. "What did they say?"

Rory tried to blank out the voices and focus on his kicking. Normally he could do that, but one word Jesse said broke his focus. "Spaznyit." The name for the surface-to-air missiles that the Russians were selling to the rebels.

Rory stood like a statue and listened, his eyes closed so he could have full concentration.

"They were pretending to be planes and making bomb noises," Jesse said. "And they did it right as we walked past."

When the other guy spoke, Rory realised it wasn't another forward at all. It was Mr Searle.

"Did you really hear that?" Mr Searle asked. "Are you sure? We need to do something about it if you did."

"Yes, sir," Jesse replied. "I heard it. They meant it."

Rory took two paces backwards and focused on the ball in front of him again. He could kick this. Even if the conversation was getting to him. Even if the way Mr Searle always agreed with Jesse got to him. Even if there were thoughts of his mum and dad in danger bursting into his mind like shrapnel, he would still kick that ball. It was what he had to do.

One step to the left, and Rory looked up, his eyes on an imaginary dot in the dead centre of the posts. The dot was in his mind first, and then it was burned into the space in the sky.

Rory breathed in.

Mr Searle's voice interrupted his calm again. "That's a disgrace," he said. "The Russian boys. It's too much. I ..."

Rory moved forwards. Three, two, one – and his foot struck the ball. The ball sailed towards the posts. Then over. Rory stood and stared at it, then heard applause from someone behind him. He saw the ball hit the spot he had burned in the sky.

The clapping might have been Mr Johnson. He had just joined in the discussion about the Russian team. His tone was friendly, but Rory knew that he was giving the assistant coach a telling-off.

"Let's not wind the boys up, shall we, Mr Searle?" Mr Johnson said. "Better we keep our minds on the match, don't you think?"

Rory marked the first kick in his notebook, then he picked up the second ball and walked 20 paces to his left. He wanted a tighter angle for his next kick.

FOUR

At the foot of the stairs, Rory took several deep breaths and listened. There were no sounds from above. That meant he had clear run without anyone else seeing what he was doing. He warmed up his legs with 12 lunges on each side – left, then right. When his muscles were stretched, he exploded up the stairs.

One breath for each set of ten steps.

That was the plan.

Two sets of ten steps per floor.

Halfway up, Rory knew he had got faster already. He might beat his record.

But at the turn for the second last floor, Rory heard a door open. He slowed down so as not to cause a crash.

A woman in a tracksuit top and shorts walked into the stairwell. David's mum. She smiled at Rory – the first smile he'd ever seen from her. He kept going, pumping his arms and legs hard up the last set of steps.

"Hey, Rory," David's mum said. "You never stop, do you?"

Rory smiled, but he was too breathless to speak.

"How long did it take you?" she asked. "Did you beat your record?"

Rory's smile was broader now. This woman knew exactly what he was doing.

"I did," he gasped. He checked his watch. "37 seconds. But my target is 35."

"That's impressive," she said. "I'm doing ten up, ten down. No time limit. No stopping either."

"That's impressive too," Rory said. He remembered David saying that his mum had run marathons. Lots of them. These steps wouldn't be a problem to her.

David's mum nodded, but the smile faded from her face.

Neither of them spoke for a few seconds.

"It takes your mind off things, doesn't it?" she said at last. "It's something to do."

"Yes," Rory said. He didn't know what to say to this woman whose husband had died in an RAF airlift only a few weeks ago. He wanted to make her feel better. But what could he say?

"Do you think about your mum out there?" David's mum asked.

"Sometimes," Rory said.

"She's a fine woman, Rory. David's dad thought the world of her."

Rory rubbed his eyes. Then he looked at David's mum.

"Are you OK?" he asked.

She nodded and smiled again. "Thanks for asking. I'm not too bad most days. It's good to be out here. I'll be on the bench with your coaches tomorrow. It'll be amazing for all you boys to play in a stadium like that, won't it?"

"It will," Rory agreed. And he left David's mum to get on with her steps.

FIVE

It was semi-final day in the Stade Mayol.

The Borderlands boys sat in the main stand, above the halfway line, where they could see the green of the pitch, the city's towering buildings and the sea beyond.

When the two teams came on, cheers and applause echoed round the stadium. Rory estimated that about a thousand people were here to watch the first semi – Scuola Como, from the north of Italy, versus Baskov School from St Petersburg, Russia. Borderlands were playing Castanet of France later.

"They're huge," Woody said, leaning into Rory. "The Baskov lads, I mean. When you see them next to the Italian lads."

Rory nodded. Woody was right – the Russian boys were massive. He suspected Baskov would use their strength and size and play a hard game.

Less than 30 seconds after kick-off, Rory was proved right. Baskov's game plan was to batter the opposition into submission. Tackles went flying in hard on anyone who had the ball. And the size of the Russian players meant that it looked like men against boys. Scuola Como took huge hits, bouncing off Baskov, hitting the ground hard.

Rory thought that the first scrum was a joke. The Russians overwhelmed the Italians no problem.

By half-time the score was astonishing. Baskov 38 – Como 9.

As the teams trooped off, two Baskov players stared up at the group from Borderlands and scowled at Jesse. Jesse glared back down at the Russian boys.

The rest of the Russian boys stopped and fixed their eyes on Jesse. Mr Johnson had to push Jesse back into his seat before the Russian team would leave the pitch.

"Jesse. Stop it," Mr Johnson said. "Use that anger on the pitch. I don't want to see any nonsense like that from Borderlands boys."

"But they're winding us up on purpose, sir," Jesse spat.

"Yes, they're winding you up," Mr Johnson said. "They want to get a rise out of you. They want to put you off your game later. But they're resorting to mind games because they're scared of us. Understand? Keep yourself under control. Don't make it easier for them."

As Mr Johnson and Jesse argued, Rory climbed out of his seat past Woody and Owen.

"Where are you going?" Owen asked.

"The pitch."

"What? Now?"

"Our game, it's an hour after this one," Rory said. "I need to kick now. There'll be no time later."

"Have you asked Mr Johnson?"

"I need to kick," Rory repeated. He walked down the stand to the metal grilles at the front, where a gate was open.

Rory knew it was a risk going onto the pitch without permission. It was half-time in a semi-final, after all. Of course it felt wrong. It felt like he was breaking a rule. But he had to overcome that feeling, because he needed to kick. Full stop. He knew the others would be looking at him and wondering if he'd lost the plot. Even Mr Johnson. But he didn't care.

Rory took a cone and placed it on the 22-metre line, level with the posts.

All the noise of arguing and the sounds of the city outside the stadium that had been so loud all through the first half faded as Rory began his routine. Six from six. Under pressure. That was what he wanted. He had ten minutes. The time pressure was good too – it would make this harder.

Rory stopped thinking. All that was there was the ball and the posts and the spot that he had burned in the air.

Two steps back. One to the left. Run up. Boot on ball.

His aim was true. Perfect.

*

The first semi-final finished Baskov 72 – Como 24.

It was a crushing defeat. Literally. Baskov School had won the game by being bigger and more brutal than the Italians. They'd given away 13 penalties and lost two players to the sin bin while they were at it. For all that, Rory had to admit that Baskov were devastating when they were running with the ball.

Rory shook his head. "That was ugly," he said. "It'll be tough if we make it to the final."

Owen and Woody agreed.

Then Mr Johnson was leaning in between them. "Minds on our game, lads. You're not in the final yet. The Russian team have been asked to clear the dressing room within 20 minutes, so I'd like to do some warm-ups on the pitch first. Shuttle runs. Stretching. OK?"

"Yes, sir," Rory said. He followed Mr Johnson down the steps and onto the pitch.

Half an hour later, Mr Johnson led his team towards their dressing room. Rory could feel match-day adrenaline rushing through his body. He still found it hard to believe they were about to play in the Toulon stadium.

But when Mr Johnson opened the door to the dressing room they heard loud music. A heavy bass. Boys singing along in rough voices.

Rory was right behind their coach as he entered and he saw 20-plus Russian players. Their kit was all over the floor. Half of them were still in towels.

"Right. Come on, lads," Mr Johnson snapped. He led his team back into the concrete corridor, where he headed towards one of the tournament organisers.

A brief discussion followed.

Rory watched. He hated this. He wanted to be in the dressing room with his head down, thinking about kicking. His nerves were jangling. He didn't need this delay. He needed to go over everything in his mind. He needed things to be like they always were. He needed to know what was going to happen next.

When Mr Johnson returned, Jesse was standing just behind Rory.

"What did they say, sir?" Jesse asked.

"There's been a ... mix-up," Mr Johnson said. "About who is using the dressing room. We'll have to get changed down the corridor. In one of the massage rooms."

Jesse pushed Rory out of the way to move forward.

"There's no mix-up, sir," he said. "They've done it on purpose. They've taken over our dressing room, like they've been taking over the countries around them for the last hundred years."

"Massage room," Mr Johnson repeated.

"Sir, we should get in there and ..."

Mr Johnson stepped towards Jesse. He towered over him. "Team Captain," he barked. "I need you to lead your team to the massage room and keep them calm and focused on the French team we have to play. Not the Russian team who have – as you put it – taken over the dressing room. Got it, Jesse? OK?"

Jesse stepped back, out of the coach's shadow. "Yes, sir," he said in a low voice. Then he turned to the team. "This way, lads."

SIX

For all that Rory thought Jesse was a complete idiot at times, he couldn't do anything but admire him during the next 80 minutes of rugby.

The Borderlands team captain was on fire.

In every play he out-thought and out-skilled the Castanet players. He made the right choice every time. To pass, to offload, to go at the French team. When he passed, he played the right team-mate in. And then he was on hand to take up the ball and storm the French line.

The French team just couldn't handle him.

Jesse's first two tries were under the posts – that made for easy conversions for Rory. His third try was an amazing double dummy run past three attempted tackles. By then the game was already won. Jesse pushed the last boy out of the way with a flat hand, then touched down on the far right side of the pitch.

Jesse's hat-trick even got the French fans on their feet.

But Rory wasn't thinking about Jesse's wonder-try – he was thinking about his own kick. This one would be harder. Much harder. It was on Rory's weaker foot and as wide as it could possibly be. It was 40 metres to the posts. A tough kick for a grown man, let alone an under-15.

For the team it didn't matter. The score was 30–9, with only a few seconds left. There was no question that Borderlands were in the final of the European Schools Trophy. But it mattered to Rory. He had put over five from five in the Stade Mayol. He wanted six from six. That would look good in his notebook. He couldn't fault himself on that.

Rory moved back two steps and took a deep breath.

Then he took one step to his left. He fixed his eyes between the posts, made his mark in the sky behind them. Breathed out. In. Then he kicked.

Some people in the stands began to applaud. They thought the ball was over. But Rory knew it wasn't. It came down just short of the crossbar. It wasn't over at all.

After the final whistle, the Castanet players formed a guard of honour and cheered Borderlands off. Rory smiled and nodded as people clapped him on the back. He knew he had to look pleased – that's what would be expected of a team of winners. But then, when everyone was off the pitch, Rory held back, waiting until all the fans had gone and both the teams were in their dressing rooms. Only Jesse was left on the pitch side. He was with a tall woman, who must be his mum – Rory had seen her at rugby matches before – and three men in suits. They were talking in French. But Rory wasn't going to worry about them.

He had something to do.

Rory picked up the match ball and walked to the spot where he'd missed his last kick.

He set the ball up on the cone, breathed in and stepped back two paces.

Breathed in.

Out.

A step to the left.

Then he stepped up to the ball and kicked.

Nobody clapped. Nobody cheered. Nobody saw. The ball hit the exact spot Rory had targeted. Just what he had wanted to do earlier.

He felt a little better. But only a little. He wanted to kick all night, try another six from six, but he could see that the floodlights around the pitch were already fading.

Back in the massage room – Borderlands' dressing room for the night – Owen and Woody looked up as Rory came in.

"Well?" Owen asked.

"Well what?" Rory said.

"Did you score?" Owen laughed. "I know why you stayed out here. You had to take that last kick again. So did you score it?"

"I did."

Rory took out his notebook. As he filled it in, Woody stood next to him.

"You missed two announcements," he said.

"Yeah? Who from?"

"Mrs Hampshire."

"What about?"

"Jesse's been offered an under-18 contract with Toulon."

Rory stared at Woody. "Really? That's amazing. Where is he?"

Woody shrugged. "I dunno."

"So what's the other announcement?" Rory asked.

"Oh, yeah ... Jesse's mum is hosting a party for the team."

"Great," Rory said. "It'll be posh. Where?"

"Very posh." Woody nodded. "It's on her yacht. The *Elite*. She's cruising the Med and she's stopped in Toulon harbour for the tournament. She's going to take us all out on the yacht for the party."

"Really?" Rory felt his stomach cramp. He closed his eyes and his thoughts began to rage out of control. He hated boats. Fathoms of water between him and the bottom of the sea. A small space with lots of people and no way off. Anything could go wrong and there'd be nothing he could do.

He would just have to think of a way to get out of the party.

As the other boys filed out of the Stade Mayol, Rory stayed behind to speak to Mr Johnson, who was checking that the Borderlands dressing room had been left tidy.

"Sir? Please can I be excused from the party on Jesse's boat?" Rory asked.

Mr Johnson looked surprised. "Why, Rory?"

"I can do some extra kicking while you're gone," Rory said. "I need the time."

Mr Johnson looked into Rory's eyes. "You're scared?" he said. "Of water?"

Rory nodded. There was no point in hiding it.

"We all have fears, Rory."

Rory nodded again. "I know," he said. He wondered what Mr Johnson was scared of.

"I want you to come," Mr Johnson said. "But I'll do you a deal. I've an idea for something that might help."

SEVEN

The next day Rory had no choice but to follow the other boys onto the boat for the party. He stuck close to Owen and Woody as they were all greeted by Jesse's mum. She looked elegant in flowing white trousers.

The engine fired and the *Elite* glided out of the harbour. Rory stood with his team-mates and looked in awe at the huge white yachts around them. Each of them had to be worth hundreds of thousands of pounds. Some were as big as buildings. In fact, they were so big that Rory wondered how they could float.

"Look at that," he heard one of the other boys say.

Rory looked and heard himself gasp. Just a few hundred metres away, several French Navy ships sat grey and menacing, low in the water. Just beyond the ships, there was an aircraft carrier. It sat there like it was the most normal thing in the world.

Once the *Elite* was out of the bay, Rory and the others went in to eat.

The dining room took up the whole of one floor of the boat. Its glass walls reflected the lights of the city and the port. Rory found it hard to believe it was all real. The boat. The meal. The bay itself.

As Rory stepped inside he saw that a big TV screen was on and they were serving a buffet. That suited Rory fine. He could grab some food and sit and watch the TV. He wanted fish or chicken – protein to feed his muscles after his last speed and strength workout on the hotel stairs. His record was 36 seconds now.

Rory sat in the only spare seat, next to David, and he and his team-mates watched TV footage of planes taking off in the dark, followed by explosions that filled the screen with yellow and orange light. Rory put down his plate – his appetite was gone.

"What's going on?" he asked David.

"Some sort of attack on Lusa – the capital of the Central Asian Republic," David said. He looked over at his mum. "Mum's had a lot of texts come in. From home. I bet she knows more than the BBC."

Rory looked across the room and studied David's mum's face. Her cheeks were pink. Her eyes were fixed on her smartphone, and one finger was tapping like fury. Taylor sat next to her, frowning at the TV screen.

"Have you asked her?" Rory said.

David looked into Rory's eyes for a moment and then shook his head. "She'll not tell us

44

anything, mate. Whatever she knows she'll tell Mr Johnson and he'll tell us if he thinks we need to know." He stood up. "But I'll tell you if she tells me, OK?"

Rory nodded. "Thanks."

David walked off and Rory looked over at Owen and Woody. They were both talking to Jesse. Jesse seemed to be shouting, like he was winding Owen up about something. Rory didn't fancy getting involved in that and so he picked up his plate and ate his food, alone. He ate on auto-pilot, not really tasting the food. David's mum smiled at him a couple of times, but she still looked on edge, and she was still reading texts. Rory imagined how hard it must be for her when the armed forces were in action like this. It must remind her of the day her husband was killed.

Rory decided to go out onto the deck. As he got up, a shout came from across the room. Jesse.

"It didn't say that," he yelled.

"It did," Owen shouted back.

Rory stared at the two boys. Their row got even louder.

"I read the sub-titles – it didn't say anything about the siege being broken!" Jesse shouted. "I know exactly what's going on. My dad texts me. And he's not told me that the siege is broken. So it isn't. OK?"

Owen looked round at the room. "I just said that the French news reported that the siege was broken," he explained. "They might be wrong. But I'm just telling you what they said."

"How do you know what they said, anyway?" Jesse's voice had changed, and there was a tone of laughter in it now. "You can't even read English, let alone French," he jeered. "Everyone knows you get special lessons."

Rory looked over at Mr Searle, who was standing with Jesse's mum. He was the only teacher in the room. He seemed to be smiling, like he thought it was OK for Jesse to say those things to Owen. Rory couldn't believe it. He should be stepping in. Now. No wonder none of the boys liked him.

"I heard what the reporter said," Owen said. "I can speak French." But his voice tailed off, like he'd run out of energy.

All the other voices in the room went silent. Mr Johnson was standing in the doorway. His eyes could have bored holes in granite.

"Jesse," Mr Johnson growled. "Outside. Now. And Mrs Hampshire – please can you join us?"

Rory slipped past Mr Johnson and out onto the deck. He didn't want to witness whatever was going to happen next. He walked round to the back of the boat. He knew there would be nobody there. Everyone was in the TV room, gripped first by the war and now by Jesse's bad behaviour.

Across the water, Toulon looked amazing. The lights of the waterfront bars and streets were reflected on the water. The angular shapes of the French fleet were ghostly shadows in the gloom. The lights of the buildings dotted over the mountainside were like little stars suspended in the sky.

Rory took this time alone to think about his parents. He wondered if they were in Cyprus, where RAF personnel often ended up. If they were, they were only a few hundred miles across the sea from here. Rory looked out into the huge black void of sea and night sky. That way. South east of here.

Then voices interrupted his thoughts.

"Let's talk here, Jesse, Mrs Hampshire," Mr Johnson said. "It's a bit more private."

Rory wondered if he should let Mr Johnson know that he was there. But it was too late. Too embarrassing. So he decided to stay still, then leave as soon as he could, before they saw him.

"I want to talk to you about what went on in there, Jesse," Mr Johnson said. "And I want your mum to be present."

"Yes, sir."

"I don't understand what the fuss is about, Mr Johnson," Jesse's mum interrupted, in the party voice she had been using since they all came on board the yacht.

Rory heard Mr Johnson breathe in like he always did when he was cross. "I just witnessed Jesse being very personal with one of the other boys, Mrs Hampshire. What Jesse said to Owen was out of order."

"He was just teasing," Mrs Hampshire said. Her voice was still light and cheerful.

"I'm afraid it was closer to bullying than teasing, Mrs Hampshire," Mr Johnson came back. "And I am sorry to say this, as we are guests on your yacht. But I must discipline the boys. Jesse, this is your last chance. We've had this talk more than once. Another episode like this and I will find another captain and consider removing you from the team."

"Well, I don't see why …" Mrs Hampshire's voice had changed. It was less playful now.

"I am responsible for all the boys," Mr Johnson said. "I could wait until we're not on your yacht, Mrs Hampshire. Or we can deal with this now."

Jesse broke in. "Mr Johnson's right, Mum. I'm sorry, sir. I was wrong to say what I said. I'll apologise to Owen as soon as I can."

"No. You shouldn't have to apologise …" Mrs Hampshire's voice tailed off.

"But I will," Jesse said. "I'll apologise." Rory heard a note of desperation in his voice.

"Good," Mr Johnson said. "Mrs Hampshire?"

Rory knew why Jesse was ready to apologise. He'd had his warning. And when Mr Johnson gave a warning like that, he meant it.

Just then, a waft of engine smoke caught in Rory's nose. He sneezed. The conversation stopped.

Rory didn't dare move. Or breathe. Was he about to be discovered? That would not be good at all.

There was a long pause. They were listening. Rory knew that.

"Mrs Hampshire," Mr Johnson said. "I'm sorry I've had to speak to your son like this when I am your guest. But he has responded well and made a good choice."

"That's no problem at all, Mr Johnson," Jesse's mum said, in her cheerful party voice again. "Shall we leave the boys to sort this out? You can join me on the bridge. You said earlier you'd like to have a go at steering the *Elite*."

EIGHT

Breakfast the next morning was quiet. The day before they'd won a European semi-final – they should be buzzing. But there was a lot else happening. The war on TV. The Russian boys winding Jesse up. Jesse winding Owen up. Being away from Borderlands. There were plenty of reasons for the boys to feel uneasy. And Rory knew that one of the main reasons was the party the night before. Some people had had a great time on the *Elite*. Others hadn't.

Mr Johnson stood up once everyone was sitting and eating. "Listen up, boys," he said. "We need to clear our heads. You agree?"

No one replied.

Mr Johnson went on regardless. "So, this morning," he said, "we're not training. We're going for a walk."

There were a couple of moans. A groan.

"Where?" a back called Thomas asked.

"You've seen that mountain behind Toulon?" Mr Johnson said. "Mont Faron."

They all nodded and mumbled, "Yes."

"We're going up that," Mr Johnson said. "At the top there's a café. Whoever makes it to the top can have a large steak and a drink on me. OK?"

It was a long, tough walk, taking over two hours. The mountain was steep and dry and rocky, with a path that dog-legged left and right all the way up.

At the start some of the lads complained but, as they walked up the rough track chat, and laughter broke out. It was warm, but not too hot, and the views were amazing. Sunlight glinted off the French fleet in the water below. At last, Rory could see that Toulon was a beautiful place. Yes, there were dual carriageways, but there were also woods and beaches and that spectacular harbour.

By the time they reached the top, Rory was buzzing.

"This is working," he said to Owen and Woody. "Loads of people are chatting. Relaxing."

"But we still need to do something about Jesse," Owen said. "Some of the other lads are blanking him. After ... you know ..."

"He deserves it," Rory said. "After what he said to you."

"Maybe," Owen said. "But that's not going to win us the final tomorrow, is it?"

The team was sitting in a café on the edge of a mountain top. There were white table cloths, bottles of water and silver cutlery catching the sun. A sheer drop fell away below the tables where they sat. They could see for miles across the sea.

Rory was pleased to be sitting opposite David's mum and sister.

"Have you broken 35 seconds yet, Rory?" David's mum asked.

"Not yet." Rory smiled, pleased she had remembered. "But I will."

"I don't doubt it," she said.

But when the steaks were finished, an uncomfortable silence settled back over the Borderlands players.

Rory watched Mr Johnson talking to Mr Searle. He could tell from their faces that they knew the team spirit had been broken – and Mr Johnson's idea for a walk had not fixed it.

But then Owen jumped to his feet. He raised his voice. "Can I say something, sir?"

Mr Johnson nodded. "Yes, Owen," he said.

Rory watched Owen take a couple of deep breaths.

"We've got a problem, Jesse," Owen said. He turned to face the team captain.

Jesse leaned back in his seat and folded his arms. "Yeah? What's that?"

Rory wondered if Owen's gamble was going to backfire. Jesse was already on the defensive.

"The problem is that we're going to lose the final tomorrow," Owen went on.

Jesse said nothing.

"We're going to lose because we've lost our team spirit," Owen said. "And that's Jesse's and my fault."

"Not yours," Thomas said.

"I don't know." Owen smiled. "But if we don't sort this, then we'll lose. You're right that Jesse wasn't at his best on the boat yesterday."

Everyone's eyes were on Jesse now. How was he going to react to that?

Owen didn't give their captain a chance to speak. "But that's Jesse," he went on. "One minute he's like that, the next he's winning us game after game. We need him. Without him, we're very good. With him, we're the best. So we have to decide. Do we want to take the

European Schools Trophy home on the flight in two days? Or do we want it to go to Russia?"

Rory saw the change in the team right away. Some of the boys were sitting up, their backs straight. They'd put their glasses down. Rory felt it inside himself too. Something powerful.

Owen turned to Jesse. "Do you want to win the trophy?" he asked.

"Course I do," Jesse said.

Owen pushed his chair back and walked over so he was face to face with Jesse. Rory saw Mr Johnson lean forward, ready to stand, in case a fight broke out.

"Two more questions?" Owen said.

"If you like."

Rory watched Jesse's hands as he bunched them into fists.

"Are we going to win this trophy if you're in the team?"

Jesse didn't hesitate. "Yeah."

"And are you sometimes an idiot – an idiot who annoys the rest of the team?"

Now Jesse did hesitate. He stalled for time with a cough, clearing his throat.

Rory stared down the mountain. It was so steep. If you slipped and fell you'd drop for ages before you hit the rocks and trees at the bottom.

At last Jesse spoke. "I suppose."

Rory noticed Mr Johnson ease back in his chair.

Owen stuck his hand out. "OK then, mate," he told Jesse. "I want to see you lift that trophy tomorrow. I want to see you in front of assembly with it back at school. I want to

see pictures of you in *Rugby World*, holding the European Schools Trophy in your idiot hands."

There was a pause. Everyone was looking from Owen to Jesse, then back again.

"So do I," Jesse said, putting his hand out too.

NINE

The squad went down Mont Faron in the cable car, in order to save their legs. And Mr Johnson kept his promise to Rory. Back at the hotel, he came to the boys' room. They were watching news footage of the war.

"Rory," said Mr Johnson. "I said if you came to the party on the boat I'd let you kick. And you did. You've got two hours. Go and kick. I've sorted it with Toulon."

Rory grabbed his kit and ran to the Toulon training ground. He was over the moon to get away from the TV. Running like this, then kicking, would help a lot.

When Rory arrived at the training ground he saw a man kicking at the far end. There was a bag of six balls and a cone waiting for Rory.

He walked out onto the main pitch, set his first ball at the near end and took out his notebook. He wrote down the date.

Six from six.

If he focused on six from six he wouldn't need to think about anything else.

Rory glanced at the man kicking at the other goal. He felt like he'd seen him before. Was he a rugby player Rory had seen on TV during the Six Nations?

Rory shook himself. This was no time for star-spotting. He had work to do.

Kick one was level with the posts. It went over perfectly.

Kick two was from ten metres left of the posts. It was perfect too.

But when he came to kick three, Rory hit trouble.

Big trouble.

Four lads came walking across the pitch out from the trees. They looked like they were making for Rory.

Rory lined up his kick and emptied his mind, trying to ignore the lads as they approached. He assumed they'd walk past, so he could kick. Just kick. That was all he wanted to do, no matter who the lads were.

But they didn't walk past him.

They stopped. They stood there and blocked the ball's flight to the posts.

Now that Rory could see them up close, he knew who they were. They were Russian players from Baskov.

Rory felt his heart rate pick up, but he focused on the ball again.

Then one of the Russians spoke.

"Spaznyit."

And something went in Rory's mind. He couldn't see the ball any more. In fact, he could see nothing but the boy who had spoken. His face. His insolent grin.

Rory went at him, two hands to the chest, hitting him with such force that the boy fell, tumbling backwards on himself. One of the other Russian lads dropped on his knees beside him. Then the other two came at Rory. The first punch hit his cheek hard and Rory felt his knees go. Another blow, to the gut, and Rory was down. Vulnerable.

Rory brought his knees into his chest just before the first kick landed. He felt a hot shaft of pain shoot from his neck, down his legs, then back again.

TEN

Rory curled into a ball as he felt the sharp pain of a kick on his back. Another jolted through his kidney.

Then he heard the shouting. At first he thought it was some abuse the Russians were throwing at him to go with the kicking. But then he realised that the words were in French.

The kicking stopped.

Rory fell on his back and opened his eyes. He was dazzled by the floodlights and didn't see the man bending over him until he felt a hand on his shoulder.

"Tu es OK?"

The touch was gentle. Not an attacker.

"Oui," Rory said, clearing his throat. He hoped it was true. "Er ... merci."

The man helped Rory to sit up.

"English?" the man asked.

"Yes ... I mean, oui."

The man laughed. "You must be careful getting up. You are perhaps injured."

"I don't think it's bad," Rory said. "I feel OK." But he took his time to stand up. He didn't want to aggravate anything that might keep him out of the final. His back felt bruised, but nothing deep. No muscle damage.

"Where did they go?" Rory asked.

"They run when I shout," the man said. "Cowards. You know them?"

Rory shook his head. "Thank you for helping me," he said. "I'm Rory. From Borderlands School. We're training here."

"I am Jean," the man said. "Jean Valjean. I am from the Rugby Club Toulon."

"What?" Rory stepped back so that he wasn't staring at the man against a floodlight, and he took a good look at him. It was Jean Valjean. *The* Jean Valjean. European Cup winner. Shorter than your average rugby player. Lean, but muscular. The French fly half.

"I've seen you," Rory said, star-struck despite himself. "You were playing for Toulon in the Heineken Cup. And for France. At Twickenham."

"Yes," Valjean said. "And I have seen you. Playing for Borderlands. In Stade Mayol. You score five from six. It is good?"

"No," Rory said in a low voice. "Not as good as six from six."

Valjean laughed. "You will never be happy, no?"

Rory smiled.

Valjean squatted to pick up the ball Rory had been about to kick. "Perhaps we train together now? I have watched you. You kick perfect. But one thing. You need to ... how you say ... kick through ...?"

"Follow through?" Rory asked.

"Yes. Follow through. Good. I show you?"

"Yes please," Rory said.

When Rory returned to the hotel he was buzzing, desperate to tell someone what had just happened. But when he got back to their floor, he saw that all his team-mates were in their common room watching the TV again. And Rory's news was nothing compared to what the TV news had to say. Owen was standing next to the screen, translating.

"The RAF has scored a victory ..." Owen said. "Erm ... after 48 hours of bombing ... the enemy ... er, rebels have retreated to positions in the mountains ... the siege of Lusa is ..."

Owen steadied himself on a chair. He grinned.

"It's over. They say ... it's a victory for the RAF. For now ..."

A massive cheer went up. Rory grinned and turned to Woody. Woody grabbed him and hugged him. He looked around and saw other boys and the adults hugging too. He wanted to cry. But he wouldn't. Not here. Not now.

Later. Only later would Rory let himself cry.

Because now he knew his parents were safe.

ELEVEN

Mr Johnson sent the boys to bed early that night. Rory understood why. For one thing, it was the night before the final and they needed the rest. But Mr Johnson also didn't want the Borderlands players walking the corridors of the hotel where they could bump into Russian players. He wanted to be safe rather than sorry.

Rory had intended to tell Mr Johnson about the attack at the training ground, but he couldn't get his coach on his own and it wasn't something he wanted to share with anyone else. It was serious, but Rory reckoned it would be better for Borderlands if no one else knew about it. Not before the final, anyway. So he kept it to himself. And because he didn't say anything about the attack, he didn't say anything about meeting Valjean either.

When Rory got into bed, he sat and looked at his notebook. He read his kicking results over the last three games he'd played in. The number of kicks he had scored and missed. He fixed on the numbers, not the feelings. Diagrams of angles and distances. It helped calm him. Rory had sensed a build-up of nerves earlier that evening in the team talk and he needed to stop it interfering with his sleep.

Owen was in the bed next to him, already asleep. His breath was slow and steady as if he had nothing to worry about at all. Rory knew he should be asleep by now too, so he reached for the light switch.

Just then, a violent crash came from the room above.

Owen sat up instantly. "Mum? What did you do that for?"

Rory smiled to himself, struggling to suppress a laugh. Woody pulled the bedcovers over his head.

There was another crash. A layer of dust dropped from the ceiling.

Then there were voices in the corridor.

Owen woke up properly. "Who's that?" he asked.

"Jesse."

Rory stood up and opened the door. Owen was right behind him.

Jesse was in the corridor, ranting. "It's the Russian team, sir," he shouted. "They're banging on the floor in every room. They're trying to keep us awake. They're trying to get to us. I reckon we go up there, sir. They want to wind us up before the game."

"And it's working, Jesse, isn't it?" Mr Johnson sighed. "Calm down and listen to me."

The boys gathered in the corridor, facing their coach, as if it was the most normal thing in the world to have a team talk at midnight in their pyjamas.

Mr Johnson shook his head, then smiled.

"Boys. We are not going to win tomorrow by being negative," he said. "We must do it by being positive. Let the Baskov lads play their stupid games. Let them exhaust themselves. We have to let it go. We have to sleep. We have to dream and remember that we are here to play rugby."

In the end, Mr Johnson agreed to go up to the Russian team's floor. The banging stopped a few minutes later. By then Rory was in bed, lights out. But he could feel the unwanted adrenaline in his system now. The Russian team's plan had worked on Jesse and it had worked on Rory too.

But Rory had a way to calm himself down. It was based on something he had learned to do to help him control his mind when he thought he might be losing it.

Rory imagined that he was at the foot of Mont Fanon in his running gear. He drew a picture in his mind of the path that weaved left then right, up to the café where the team had eaten steak earlier in the day.

Then Rory began to run up the path, in his mind. The cable car whirred over him and the hot air cooled as he climbed higher and higher. He imagined the crumbling stone path, the French Navy fleet in the distance, the sun rising. Warmth on his skin as he ran at a steady pace up the hill.

Rory was asleep in minutes.

TWELVE

The Stade Félix Mayol. Toulon. Home of one of the finest – and richest – teams in European rugby. Four huge stands. A perfect rectangle of pitch. And a deep blue French sky.

It was the first scrum in the final of the European Schools Trophy.

As soon as Jesse took the ball from the feet of Danny, the Borderlands number 8, two huge Russian boys targeted him. They hit him hard. Flattened him.

Penalty to Borderlands, deep in their own half.

Rory kicked the ball into touch, just over the halfway line, and gained them 30 metres.

The lineout that followed became a maul, then the referee called for a scrum.

And it happened again. The Russian boys smashed Jesse, the moment his hands were on the ball.

A Baskov player was warned.

Another penalty. 35 metres out.

Rory understood the Russian game plan. They knew that Jesse was the Borderlands playmaker and they would batter him. They'd give away penalties all day – as long as they thought the kicks were out of Rory's range. And as long as they thought they could put Jesse out of action.

Jesse shook his head and picked up the ball.

"I'll kick it," Rory said.

"Too far," Jesse said. "You'll miss."

"They'll smash you all day if we don't start punishing them for it, Jesse."

Rory watched as Jesse thought.

"Can you do it?" Jesse asked at last.

"Yes," Rory said.

And he could. He would. There was no other thought in his head – and no point in thinking anything else. The ball had to go on the cone, off his boot and between the posts. He'd already seen it happen in his mind. No matter that it was beyond the usual range of an under-15 player. He could do it.

Rory heard some of the Baskov players laughing when he set the ball down on the cone. He ignored them. They could goad him all they liked. They wouldn't get to him. Not while he was on the field of play.

Rory flexed his leg muscles. "I can do this," he told himself. "My legs are stronger now. I've got better technique." The stair runs had helped. As had the follow-through tips from Jean Valjean. They'd give his kicks an extra ten metres, if he believed in himself. And he did believe.

Rory stepped back two paces, then one to the side. He breathed in, then out. Closed his eyes, then opened them. He was alone on the pitch. Just him, the ball, the posts.

Then he stepped up, kicked and followed through – forcing his leg right through the kick.

An echo of his boot striking the ball came back off one of the buildings around the stadium.

It sounded bizarre.

But Rory knew that the ball was over the moment he hit it.

He closed his eyes again, felt a hand on his shoulder. Then Woody's voice said, "Fantastic, Rory."

And Rory knew he'd done something special. He'd found those extra metres on his kicking. Maybe an extra ten. Now he could really get at the Russian team.

The rest of the first half was tough.

Baskov didn't let up their aggressive game. They had a player sin-binned after 11 minutes, then another after 27. But Borderlands still struggled to make ground. Rory could see that his team-mates were rattled. Their normal fluent passing was absent. They made mistakes, especially in their own half.

By half-time Borderlands had given away nine penalties. The Baskov fly half had scored three of them.

And despite all the foul play, the Russians had given away only three kickable penalties.

Rory had slotted away all three.

9–9.

Half-time.

Rory watched the Baskov players jog off the pitch as soon as their captain had kicked the ball into touch. They seemed to have a lot of energy left. Then Rory watched his own team-mates. Their heads were down, their legs heavy – they looked tired. Some seemed to be carrying minor injuries. It had been a battle – a war. And it was clear which team felt it was winning.

THIRTEEN

The second half was the hardest 40 minutes of rugby Rory had ever played. He could feel it in his muscles. He felt weak when he tried to run with the ball and pass it. He had never felt like this before in a game of rugby. His body was spent. And his mind wasn't far behind it.

He could see that the same was true of his team-mates. And of the Russian team, too.

Everything was slower. Harder work. More careless mistakes. As a result, there were more penalties – seven more. Rory had kicked his two. The Russian fly half had scored one of his five.

It was 15–12 to Borderlands, with minutes to go.

It was hard to believe Borderlands were that close to winning. But Rory knew he had to focus on each play, not on the final score. And not on the trophy.

Rory had been watching the Baskov fly half. He could see that his legs were going. He was refusing kicks over 25 metres now.

Another scrum.

Borderlands had the feed.

Rory heard Jesse shouting. "Possession. Keep possession." Then he tapped the ball on one of the prop's shoulders and fed the scrum.

But the scrum bit back. The Baskov pack had more in their legs after all. And the Borderlands pack was struggling. Rory watched

Jesse panic and join the flanker in the maul for the ball along with Rahim and George.

Rory stepped back. They were strung out now. If the Russians got the ball away cleanly ...

He broke off this thought before it finished. The Russian scrum half was firing a fast ball ten metres across to his line of backs.

Baskov had six men on Borderlands' four.

One more pass and it was four on two.

Rory ran as hard as he could to grab at the boy with the ball. His arms slipped down the player's knees, then his calves. Rory felt the Baskov winger's boot catch his face. He'd missed the tackle.

The roar of the Russian players – and the shouts from the crowd – told Rory all he needed to know.

Try.

The unthinkable.

17–15 to Baskov. And a kick to come.

As the Russian fly half lined up the kick,
Rory stood up and ran over to Jesse. He had
to let his captain know that the Russian kicker
was losing range.

"Jesse?" he shouted.

But Jesse wasn't listening. He was staring
at the blocks of flats that crowded the sky
north of the Stade Mayol.

"Jesse!"

"What?" Jesse's voice was angry. It was the
tone of a defeated captain, no question.

Rory watched David go up to Jesse and push
him to bring him to.

"Listen!" David shouted. "It's critical. Listen to Rory."

At last Rory had his captain's attention. Only David could have done that.

"He'll miss the kick," Rory said. "He's lost his range. He'll kick it short. We'll get possession. You need to get us as close to their 22 as you can. With possession. We've got a minute. For the drop goal."

"What?" Jesse looked confused.

"The drop goal," Rory said. "I need the ball this side of the 22. Understand? He's. Going. To. Miss. This. Kick. Get everyone ready under the posts. It'll fall short."

The boys went quiet as they watched the Baskov fly half set up the kick. Jesse lined the backs up as Rory had told him.

They watched the fly half run up hard and strike the ball.

"Too much," Rory said, before he'd even touched it.

And Rory was right. The fly half hit the ball hard. Very hard. But his aim was way off.

And Owen was under it, wide on the left. Owen tossed it to Woody. Woody the battering ram. Woody ran hard. He dodged three tackles, making it to the halfway line before the shattered Russians brought him down.

Sixty seconds on the clock.

Borderlands had to play it fast.

Two phases later, Borderlands had the ball on the Baskov 22.

A scrum.

Rory stood back, breathing deeply. He wanted as much oxygen as possible – in his lungs, in his muscles, in his blood.

This was it. The moment of truth.

Rory watched Jesse urge the pack on. Shout at them. They had to win this scrum. Then Jesse had to get the ball back to Rory.

Another deep breath. Rory needed the power in his legs.

The scrum went down. Rory heard the two packs slap against each other. He watched the legs of the two props, their thighs pushing on, their studs ripping up the famous pitch of the Stade Mayol.

Then he saw the ball, a fleck of white moving through the forest of legs.

Into Jesse's hands.

FOURTEEN

Rory watched Jesse as his hands hovered over the ball at the back of the scrum.

Then Jesse looked over his shoulder. Right into Rory's eyes.

Rory mouthed, "Yes."

Jesse's hands were on the ball now. He was looking down. Then he twisted his body, his arms going forward. A flick of his wrists and the ball was coming at Rory.

It was spinning. Light coming off it.

Rory changed the position of his feet. He felt the ball in his hands.

He looked up.

Five Russian players were coming at him.

He knew two of them. They were his attackers from the night before.

But they were too late. They might get Rory, but they wouldn't get the ball.

The ball fell from Rory's hands.

It hit the ground as he swung his foot.

Contact.

Rory made sure that he followed through. Just like Jean Valjean had shown him. He gave it everything. Then he fell, just as two of the Baskov players hit him.

But Rory felt no pain. He didn't care about them – he knew the ball was up and away. And he knew that it was over.

Three points for the drop goal.

Borderlands 18. Baskov 17.

There was a scuffle above Rory as he lay on the ground.

Then the whistle.

It was over.

Borderlands were the Champions of Europe.

Rory felt arms around him, then his legs go, bodies on top of him. There were shouts. Cheers. Slaps on Rory's back, his shoulders, his head. He felt drained. He wasn't sure he'd be able to pick up a ball now, let alone kick one.

But as he lay there, Rory felt OK. He couldn't move, but he was OK. Like he was finally satisfied.

And the thing that made him feel the most OK – the thing that was buzzing through his body – was that he had six from six. Five penalty attempts and a drop goal. All of them over the posts.

He hoped Jean Valjean was in the stadium to see it.

Rory stood next to Owen and Woody as they watched their team captain step up to collect the European Schools Rugby Trophy.

The players from the three other teams stood on either side of the small stage, but Jesse didn't look at them as he approached. He stepped up onto the stage and took the trophy in both hands, then turned and lifted it.

A huge cheer echoed through the Stade Mayol. Most of the other players were cheering and clapping. And there were still several hundred people in the main stand. Rory spotted Jesse's mum, and David's mum and sister. All of them waving and grinning.

When Jesse brought the trophy over to the rest of the team, he walked just a fraction too close to the Russian players. Rory saw how he glared into each of the Baskov players' eyes, saying nothing. The Russian boys looked furious, but none of them reacted.

Rory shook his head. Jesse just couldn't help himself. He couldn't let things lie. Maybe that was what made him such a brilliant player.

Woody interrupted Rory's thoughts. "We're European champions. I can't believe it," he said. "Do you reckon we're going to get a medal?"

Owen shoved Woody with his shoulder. "Not all of us. But there is a Player of the Tournament award."

"Jesse might as well have stayed on the stage then," Rory said.

Owen and Woody laughed.

"Can you believe we're in the World Finals now?" Woody said. "New Zealand. Amazing."

Rory shuddered at the thought of 28 hours of travel on a plane. He didn't fancy that at all. But he knew he wasn't supposed to worry about the future. He was meant to enjoy the moment today.

Then he saw Jean Valjean.

The French International stood on stage next to the official who'd given Jesse the trophy. So Jesse was going to receive his Player of the Tournament award from Valjean. Wow! Rory hoped Jesse would recognise him.

"And now it is time to award the Player of the Tournament medal," the official announced.

Rory watched Jesse hand the trophy to David.

"Jean Valjean has kindly agreed to award it," the official went on.

There was a cheer from the crowd. Valjean was one of their big heroes.

"The winner of the Player of the Tournament medal is ..." Jean Valjean hesitated as he read the piece of paper he'd been handed, then a smile broke out across his face. He looked at Rory. "Is ... Rory Samsudin!"

Rory stared at Jean Valjean. Had he heard him right?

"Yes, you," Valjean said into his microphone. "You kick six from six. It is perfect, no?"

So Rory walked up to collect his award. He took Valjean's hand and shook it.

"Thank you," he said.

"No problem." Jean Valjean grinned. "Congratulations."

Then Rory turned round to face his team-mates. He raised the award – not above his head, just a slight raise to say thank you to his team-mates, who were all clapping and smiling.

Even Jesse was clapping. In fact, Jesse's grin was the biggest of all. He was the captain who had led his team to the World Schools Trophy finals in New Zealand. He was the star player, who'd been talent-spotted for a contract with Toulon. And he was a good enough captain to know he couldn't have done it without Rory.

As he held the award, Rory knew that all his training had paid off. Right at the end, he'd kept his head and put Jean Valjean's expert tips into practice – and kicked the six from six he so desperately wanted to kick.

But now the game was over, Rory wanted the pitch to clear. He wanted the fans to leave. The officials. The Baskov players. Even the Borderlands lot. He wanted to be alone on this perfect green pitch. Just him and a bag of six balls. He wanted six from six. Again.

Rory knew that this was only the beginning.

ACKNOWLEDGEMENTS

Big thanks are due to my wife and daughter and to my agent, David Luxton. To Ali Taft, Anna Turner and James Nash at our writing group. To Jude Gibbon in Basildon. To Mr Auckland and everyone at Albrighton Primary School, where many children have parents based at RAF Cosford. Thanks to Steven Price and his son Theo for their rugby union expertise. To Phil Craxford and his son Lucas, who ran up and down a hotel staircase, so I could get Rory's efforts right. To Barrington Stoke for their hard work and inspiration.

I researched *Surface to Air* in Toulon in 2013. Huge thanks to Andrew Sheridan for showing me round the Stade Mayol and for letting me watch the team train. Thanks to Jonny Wilkinson for *Jonny: My Autobiography* – the best sports autobiography I've read. And I've read a few.

Our books are tested
for children and young people by
children and young people.

Thanks to everyone who consulted on
a manuscript for their time and effort in
helping us to make our books better
for our readers.